CW00867013
THE 7 DAYS
A Classic Nursery Rhyme Made New
Every Child in the World
is Born On One of Seven Days-
What Does Your Day
Say About You?
Written by
Deborah Burns
Illustrated by
Cydney Bittner

The 7 Days

DJB Ventures LLC
Velvet Hammer Press
Baldwin, New York

Library of Congress Control Number: 2022915904
ISBN
softcover 978-1-7368580-3-5
hardcover 978-1-7368580-4-2
digital 978-1-7368580-5-9


To get a downloadable, printable Keepsake PDF, just email contactdbauthor@gmail.com and it will be on its way.

THIS BOOK
BELONGS TO:

Moon

# DAY 1

## MONDAY'S CHILD

EMOTIONAL.
INTUITIVE.
COMMUNICATIVE.

"Which day of the week was
I born on, Mommy?" Emilia asks.

"Every child comes into the world on
one of just seven days," her mother answers.

"And you were born on a Monday, which tells
me a lot about you.

"Monday's Child is knowing and sure,
sparkling with light and words so pure,"
her mother rhymes.

"That sounds like me!" Emilia laughs.

"Yes, it does," her mother agrees.
"And I love all those things about you!"

Mars

# DAY 2
# TUESDAY'S CHILD

ENERGETIC.
SPIRITED.
HONORABLE.

"Which day of the week was my 'birth' day Mama?" Horado wonders.

"Well, there's only one day for you!"
his mother replies.

"Tuesday's Child is playful and bold,
glowing with fire and a spirit of gold."

"You were definitely born on a Tuesday!" his mother beams.

"Hurray," cheers Horado. "I am a Tuesday's Child from my head to my toes!"

Mercury

# DAY 3
# WEDNESDAY'S CHILD

INTELLECTUAL.
OPTIMISTIC.
MINDFUL.

"When did my story begin, Mum? Which day of the week is mine?" Pippa whispers.

"You were born on a Wednesday, my dearest one.

"Wednesday's Child is worldly and wise,
brimming with joy and dreams that rise,"
her mother sing-songs.

"That really does describe me!" Pippa giggles.

"It most certainly does. You are a Wednesday's Child through-and-through," her mother responds.

Jupiter

# DAY 4
## THURSDAY'S CHILD

GENEROUS.
SOCIAL.
ABUNDANT.

"Do you remember the day of the week I was born, Mata?" Anya asks.

"Of course I do, my daughter!
You were gifted to me on a Thursday.

"Thursday's Child is kind and giving,
juggling good causes with peaceful living,"
her mother announces.

"Well, that definitely sums me up!"
Aanya chuckles.

"These words have described you
from the start," her mother confirms.

Venus

# DAY 5
## FRIDAY'S CHILD

ARTISTIC.
WHIMSICAL.
CARING.

"Which day of the week was it when you first met me, Muma?" Deaven wants to know.

"I will never forget looking into your eyes for the first time on a Friday," his mother recalls.

"Friday's Child is creative and true, bursting with love and great ideas too."

"That's me, that's me!" Deaven exclaims.

"Without a doubt, you are a Friday's Child," his mother assures.

Saturn

# DAY 6
## SATURDAY'S CHILD

PERCEPTIVE.
HOPEFUL.
DETERMINED.

"On which day of the week did I first appear, Mère?" Sabine inquires.

"Ah, my chouchou, I will never forget that Saturday!

"Saturday's Child is lively and smart,
blazing new trails and working with heart,"
her mother recites.

"I am very much like that," Sabine pronounces.

"Yes, you absolutely are!" her mother coos.

Sun

# DAY 7
## SUNDAY'S CHILD

REFLECTIVE.
HONEST.
RESPECTFUL.

"When did I arrive in the world?
Which day was it, Haha?" Jiro asks.

"My treasure, you were born on a Sunday.

"Sunday's Child is considerate and fair,
blessed with truth and ideals so rare,"
his mother declares.

"That makes me feel so special!" Jiro smiles.

"It should, for you are all of those things and more," his mother nods.

"Please tell me the whole rhyme for all the days," Emilia begs her mother.

Smiling, her mother recites:

"Monday's Child is knowing and sure,
sparkling with light and words so pure,

Tuesday's Child is playful and bold,
glowing with fire and a spirit of gold,

Wednesday's Child is worldly and wise,
brimming with joy and dreams that rise,

Thursday's Child is kind and giving,
juggling good causes with peaceful living,

Friday's Child is creative and true,
bursting with love and great ideas too,

Saturday's Child is lively and smart,
blazing new trails and working with heart,

Sunday's Child is considerate and fair,
blessed with truth and ideals so rare."

"But ..." Emilia pauses. "Could I have a little bit of all the days in me?"

"You do!" her mother says. "Children everywhere in the world are born with their day's talents - and with some of the strengths from the other six days too."

"That connects us all together!" Emilia realizes.

"Yes, my darling.

"We all have everything we will ever need already inside of us, forever and ever,"
her mother promises.

THE END OF THE STORY

AND THE BEGINNING OF YOURS ...

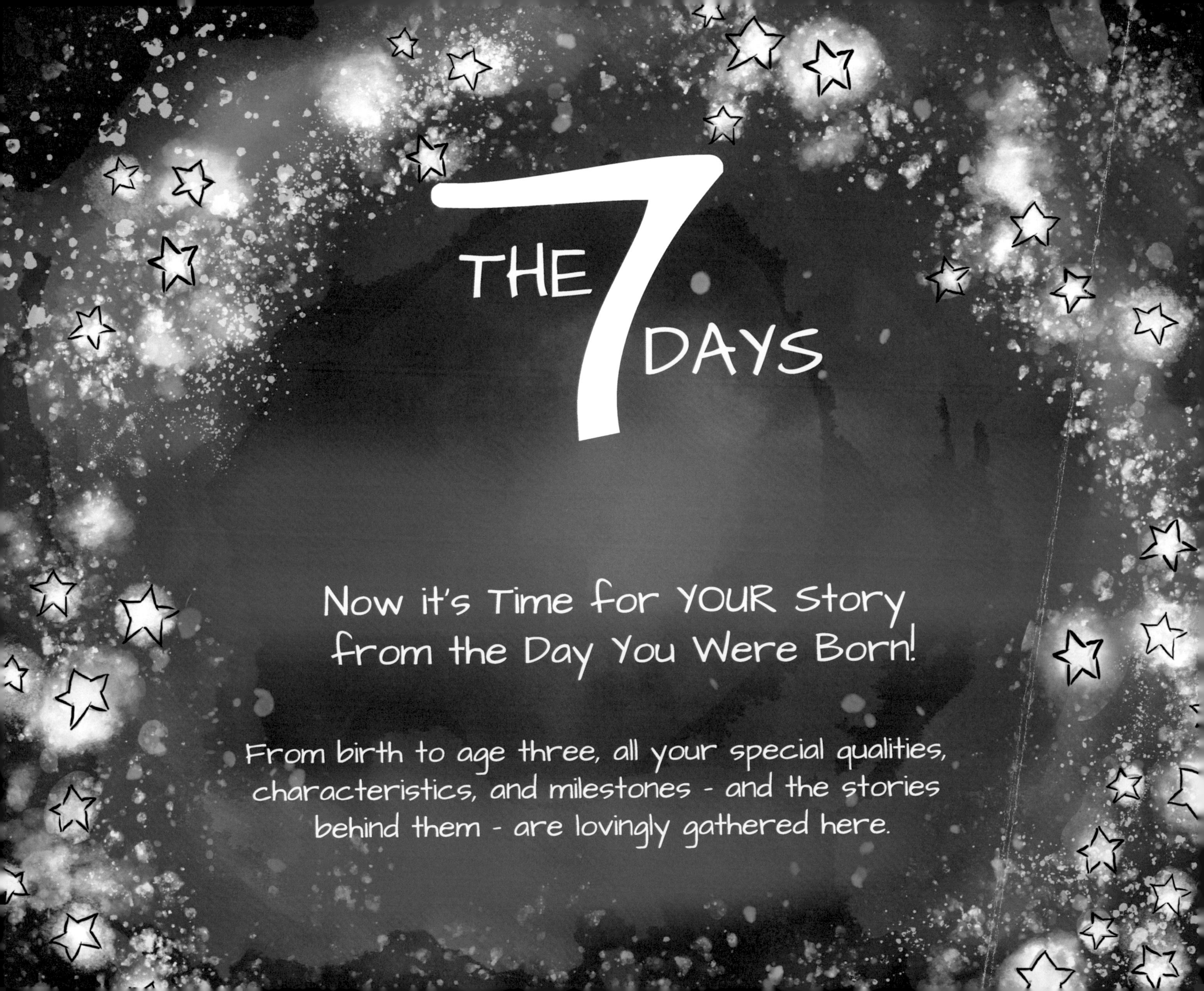
THE 7 DAYS
Now it's Time for YOUR Story
from the Day You Were Born!
From birth to age three, all your special qualities,
characteristics, and milestones - and the stories
behind them - are lovingly gathered here.

# MY ARRIVAL INTO THE WORLD

MY NAME IS:

I WAS BORN ON A:

MY DAY'S THREE STRENGTHS:

MY DAY'S RHYMING LINE:

WHAT'S MY BIRTH STORY?

WAS THERE ANYTHING FUNNY OR UNUSUAL OR UNEXPECTED?

HOW DID YOU FEEL WHEN YOU FIRST SAW ME?

WHO DID I RESEMBLE THE MOST?

WHY DID YOU CHOOSE MY NAME, AND DOES IT HAVE A SPECIAL MEANING?

WHAT IS ONE THING YOU WILL NEVER FORGET ABOUT THE DAY I WAS BORN?

WHO WERE MY FIRST VISITORS, AND WHAT DID THEY SAY ABOUT ME?

WHAT IS YOUR BIGGEST WISH FOR ME?

WHO AND WHAT DO YOU PREDICT I'LL BE WHEN I GROW UP?

# MY FIRST THREE YEARS

ANSWERS TO THE SAME QUESTIONS
OVER TIME SHOW CHANGE,
GROWTH, AND MINDSET.

# FIRST BIRTHDAY

WHICH OF MY DAY'S THREE STRENGTHS ARE THE STRONGEST IN ME, AND HOW DO I EXPRESS THEM?

HOW DO MY EMOTIONS, ACTIONS, AND RESPONSES DEMONSTRATE MY DAY'S RHYME?

WHICH TRAITS FROM THE OTHER DAYS OF THE WEEK ARE ALSO STRONG IN ME?

WHAT ARE MY INTERESTS AND FAVORITE ACTIVITIES?

WHAT IS MOST UNIQUE ABOUT ME?

## SECOND BIRTHDAY

NOW, WHICH OF MY DAY'S THREE STRENGTHS ARE THE STRONGEST IN ME, AND HOW DO I EXPRESS THEM?

HOW DO MY EMOTIONS, ACTIONS, AND RESPONSES DEMONSTRATE MY DAY'S RHYME?

WHICH TRAITS FROM THE OTHER DAYS OF THE WEEK ARE ALSO STRONG IN ME?

WHAT ARE MY INTERESTS AND FAVORITE ACTIVITIES?

WHAT IS MOST UNIQUE ABOUT ME?

# THIRD BIRTHDAY

NOW, WHICH OF MY DAY'S THREE STRENGTHS ARE THE STRONGEST IN ME, AND HOW DO I EXPRESS THEM?

HOW DO MY EMOTIONS, ACTIONS, AND RESPONSES DEMONSTRATE MY DAY'S RHYME?

WHICH TRAITS FROM THE OTHER DAYS OF THE WEEK ARE ALSO STRONG IN ME?

WHAT ARE MY INTERESTS AND FAVORITE ACTIVITIES?

WHAT IS MOST UNIQUE ABOUT ME?

# ACKNOWLEDGMENTS

This book is inspired by the traditional nineteenth-century nursery rhyme, "Monday's Child" (public domain; author unknown):

"Monday's Child is fair of face,
Tuesday's Child is full of grace,
Wednesday's Child is full of woe,
Thursday's Child has far to go,
Friday's Child is loving and giving,
Saturday's Child works hard for a living,
And the child that is born on the Sabbath day is bonny and blithe and good and gay."

I was born on a Saturday and this nursery rhyme has always held great meaning for me. In fact, "Saturday's Child" became the name of my award-winning memoir about my mother and our relationship. And as I explained its title to generations of women, it became clear that the popularity of the original nursery rhyme was sadly dwindling. So, I went down a new path that led me to this book that you hold in your hands.

Its message is important because every single person in this world - no matter how near or how far; how similar or how different - is born on one of just seven days.

Now, I hope that this retelling for a new era - which adds the dimension of the ruling planets, colorways, and animals assigned to each day from both astrology and mythology - will enhance the meaning of every child's special day and connect children everywhere to one another.

## AUTHOR BIO

Deborah Burns loves inspiring others to see possibilities and opportunities. Connecting the dots and building ideas is her hallmark, whether as a media chief innovation officer, a consultant helping companies invent and reinvent, or as the author of two award-winning books: "Authorize It! Think Like a Writer to Win at Work & Life" and "Saturday's Child." Now, "THE 7 DAYS" connects the dots in her own life as she reinvents the classic nursery rhyme that has a place of honor in "Saturday's Child." And now, as she enters the children's book genre - and enjoys her new role as the grandmother of two little girls - she looks forward to all the possibilities ahead.

## ILLUSTRATOR BIO

Cydney Bittner received a B.A. in Studio Art and Illustration & Animation from Marymount Manhattan College. In addition to her illustration work, she has worked as an art instructor in her hometown of Bucks County, Pennsylvania. In her experience teaching, she has seen firsthand the importance of imagination; she strives to create art that nurtures that critical part of the human psyche. This is Cydney's third children's book, following "Libby the Ladybug Learns Helpfulness" by Carly Furino, and "George the Alligator" by Margaret Sansom.

Lightning Source UK Ltd.
Milton Keynes UK
UKRC032300101022
410273UK00005B/12